Puffin Books
Editor: Kaye Webb

The Spider's Palace
and Other Stories

The best thing about modern fairy tales is
that they are always so surprising, especially
when, as with this collection, they are written
by the author of *A High Wind In Jamaica*.

What would be better than a story about a
little girl who travels by telephone, just
slipping quietly down the wires whenever she
wants to visit friends without her step-parents
knowing ... (although rather alarming
when you arrive at the wrong number by
mistake). And what about going to live
inside a w'ale or attending a mouse party in
an upside-down house, or having a magic
eye-glass which turns people into toys? Then
there is the boy who makes everything dark
until he stands on his head, and a gardener
who chases a magic rabbit who commands a
team of white elephants – the more extraordinary and even alarming it is, the more
likely you are to find it inside *The Spider's
Palace*.

For seven-, eight- and nine-year-olds.

Cover design by Erik Blegvad

D0552352

He shouted to the captain of a ship to give him a pill

RICHARD HUGHES

The Spider's Palace

and other stories

WITH ILLUSTRATIONS BY
GEORGE CHARLTON

PUFFIN BOOKS

Puffin Books, Penguin Books Ltd,
Harmondsworth, Middlesex, England
Penguin Books Australia Ltd, Ringwood, Victoria, Australia
Penguin Books (N.Z.) Ltd, 182–190 Wairau Road, Auckland 10, New Zealand

—

First published by Chatto and Windus 1931
Published in Puffin Books 1972
Reprinted 1973, 1974, 1976

—

Copyright © Richard Hughes, 1960

—

Made and printed in Great Britain by
Cox & Wyman Ltd, London, Reading and Fakenham
Set in Intertype Baskerville

Contents

Living in W'ales

Living in W'ales

Once there was a man who said he didn't like the sort of houses people lived in, so he built a model village. It was not really like a model village at all, because the houses were all big enough for real people to live in, and he went about telling people to come and Live in W'ales.

There was also living in Liverpool a little girl who was very nice. So when all the people went off with the man to live in W'ales, she went with them. But the man walked so fast that presently some of them got left behind. The ones who were left behind were the little girl, and an Alsatian dog, and a very cross old lady in a bonnet and black beads, who was all stiff, but had a nice husband, who was left behind too.

So they went along till they came to the sea; and in the sea was a whale. The little girl said, 'That was what he meant, I suppose, when he talked about living in W'ales. I expect the others are inside: or, if not, they are in another one. We had better get in this one.'

So they shouted to know if they might come in, but the whale didn't hear them. The nice husband said that if that was what living in W'ales meant, he would rather go back to Liverpool: but the horrid old lady said, 'Nonsense! I will go and whisper in its ear.'

But she was very silly, and so instead of whispering in its ear she went and tried to whisper in its blowhole. Still the whale didn't hear; so she got very cross and said, 'None of this nonsense, now! Let us in at once! I won't have it, do you hear? I simply won't stand it!' and she began to stir in his blowhole with her umbrella.

So the whale blew, like an enormous sneeze, and blew her right away up into the sky on top of the water he blew out of his hole, and she was never seen again. So then the nice husband went quietly back to Liverpool.

But the little girl went to the whale's real ear, which was very small and not a bit like his blowhole, and whispered into it, 'Please, nice whale, we would so like to come in, if we may, and live inside.' Then the whale opened his mouth, and the little girl and the Alsatian dog went in.

When they got right down inside, of course, there was no furniture. 'He was quite right,' said the little girl. 'It is certainly not a bit like living in a house.'

The only thing in there was a giant's wig that the whale had once eaten. So the little girl said, 'This will do for a door mat.' So she made it into a door mat, and the Alsatian dog went to sleep on it.

When he woke up again he started to dig holes: and of course it gave the whale most terrible pains to have holes dug by such a big dog in his inside, so he went up to the top of the water and shouted to the captain of a ship to give him a pill. On board the ship there was a cold dressed leg of mutton that the captain was tired of, so he thought, 'That will make a splendid pill to give the whale.' So he

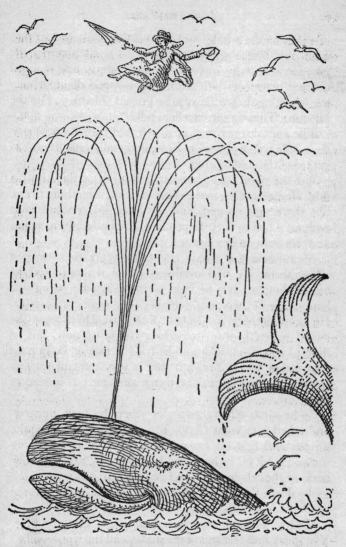

. . . And she was never seen again

threw it to the whale, and the whale swallowed it; and when it came tobogganing down the whale's throat the Alsatian dog, who was very hungry, ate it, and stopped digging holes: and when the dog stopped digging holes the whale's pain went away. So he said 'Thank you' to the captain: 'That was an excellent pill.'

The captain was very surprised that his pill had made the whale well again so soon: he had really only done it to get rid of the cold mutton.

But the poor little girl wasn't so lucky as the Alsatian dog. *He* had a door mat to sleep on, and something to eat. But there was no bed, and the little girl couldn't sleep without a bed to sleep on possibly, and had nothing to eat, and this went on for days and days.

Meanwhile the whale began to get rather worried about them. He had swallowed them without thinking much about it; but he soon began to wonder what was happening to them, and whether they were comfortable. He knew nothing at all about little girls. He thought she would probably want something to eat by now, but he didn't know at all what. So he tried to talk down into his own inside, to ask her. But that is very difficult: at any rate *he* couldn't do it. The words all came out instead of going in.

So he swam off to the tropics, where he knew a parrot, and asked him what to do. The parrot said it was quite simple, and flew off to an island where there was a big snake. He bit off its head and bit off its tail, and then flew back to the whale with the rest of it. He put most of the snake down the whale's throat, so that one end just came up out of its mouth.

'There,' he said, 'now you have got a speaking tube. You speak into one end of the snake, and the words will go down it inside you.'

So the whale said 'Hallo' into one end of the snake, and the little girl heard 'Hallo' come out of the other. 'What do you want?' said the whale. 'I want something to eat,' said the little girl. The whale told the parrot, 'She wants something to eat. What do little girls eat?'

'Little girls eat rice pudding,' said the parrot. He had one, in a big glass bowl: so he poured it down the snake too, and it came down the other end and the little girl ate it.

When she had eaten it she caught hold of her end of the snake, and called 'Hallo!' up it.

'Hallo!' said the whale.

'May I have a bed?' said the little girl.

'She wants a bed,' the whale said to the parrot.

'You go to Harrods for that,' said the parrot, 'which is the biggest shop in London,' and flew away.

When the whale got to Harrods, he went inside. One of the shopwalkers came up to him and said, 'What can I do for *you*, please?' which sounded very silly.

'I want a bed,' said the whale.

'Mr Binks, BEDS!' The shopwalker called out very loud, and then ran away. He was terribly frightened, because there had never been a whale in the shop before.

Mr Binks The Bed Man came up and looked rather worried.

'I don't know that we have got a bed that will exactly fit you, sir,' he said.

'Why not, silly?' said the whale. 'I only want an ordinary one.'

'Yes, sir,' said the Bed Man, 'but it will have to be rather a large ordinary one, won't it?'

'Of course not, silly,' said the whale. 'On the contrary, it will have to be rather a small one.'

He saw a very nice little one standing in a corner.

'I think that one will just about fit me,' he said.

'You can have it if you like,' said the Bed Man. 'But I think it's you who are the silly to think a little bed like that will fit you!'

'I want it to fit me *inside*, of course,' said the whale, 'not *outside*! – Push!' and he opened his mouth.

So they all came and pushed, and sure enough it just did fit him. Then he ate all the pillows and blankets he could find, which was far more than was needed really, and when it all got down inside, the little girl made the bed and went to sleep on it.

So the whale went back to the sea. Now that the little girl and the Alsatian dog both had had something to eat and somewhere to sleep, they said:

'The man was right; it really is much more fun living in W'ales than living in houses.'

So they stayed on.

P.S. – The parrot went on feeding them, not always on rice pudding.

The Dark Child

The Dark Child

In a big house at one end of a village there used to live a very large family. There were so many children that it was very lucky it was a big house. Now the curious thing was that all these children were fair as fair could be, except one; and he wasn't just dark, he was black.

He wasn't just black like a Negro, either: he was much blacker than that; he was black in the same way the night is: in fact, he was so black that anyone anywhere near him could hardly see anything. Just as a lamp gives out light, he gave out dark – and his name was Joey.

One morning poor Joey came into the nursery where all his brothers and sisters were playing.

'Oh, Joey, dear, *please* go away. We can't see to play,' they all said together.

So, very sad, poor Joey went downstairs and into the library, where his father sat reading his paper.

'Hallo!' said his father without looking up. 'Dark morning, what? Hardly see to read!'

Then he looked round and saw Joey.

'That you, my boy? Run away now, like a good little chap. Father's busy.'

So, sadder still, Joey went out into the garden. It was a lovely sunny morning, and he wandered down to the fruit garden and stopped to think. Presently he heard the gardener's voice:

'Now then, Master Joey, how do you think my peaches is ever going to ripen, if you stand there keeping the sun off them?'

Poor Joey began to cry quietly to himself. 'The only thing to do,' he thought, 'is to run away; I see that.'

So he ran away, all down the village. But before he got to the far end, a nice brown spaniel came out of a garden to see why it was so dark outside: and just then, too, a motor came along. When he got into Joey's dark the driver couldn't see the dog, and ran over it; but he didn't kill it, he only hurt one of its legs.

When the motor had gone on, Joey went out and picked up the dog, and carried it to its house.

'That was *my* fault,' he thought, 'for making the dark.'

Someone opened the door and, very surprised, took the dog in, and Joey went away. But while this was happening, a little girl who lived in the house looked out of the window. She was astonished to see that it was almost night in the garden below, but she could just see something black moving about in the middle of it.

'I must go and see what that is,' she said, 'and I mustn't forget my magic grain of rice.'

So she took a very secret matchbox that she kept hidden behind the clock, and opened it: and inside there was nothing but a single grain of rice. This she took out and put in her mouth, just inside her underlip, between that and her teeth, so that anything she said would have to come out over the magic grain of rice. The advantage of this was that whatever the little girl tried to say, only the truth could come out over the grain of rice; and that happened even if it was something the little girl didn't herself know. If you asked her a question about something she had never heard of, even, if she had the grain of rice inside her lip she always gave the right answer.

She had often found it useful in school.

So she followed Joey down the road (though keeping outside his dark herself) and into a field. There he stopped, and she spoke to him.

What she tried to say was, 'Who are you, black boy, that make such a dark? I *am* frightened of you': but what came out (because of the grain of rice) was, '*Poor* Joey! I *am* sorry for you!'

When he heard himself spoken to like that, of course he was ever so pleased.

'How do you know who I am?' he asked. 'I have never been down the village before, because I didn't want people to know about me.'

The little girl tried to answer, 'I don't know,' but what she actually said was, 'Of course I know!'

'Then can you help me?' asked Joey. 'Can you tell me what to do so as not to be so dark?'

The little girl tried to say, 'I'm afraid I can't,' but what she *did* say was, 'Of course I can! Try standing on your hands instead of your feet.'

'I don't know how,' said Joey: so she helped him stand on his hands against a haystack. The change was sudden and wonderful: for no sooner did he stand on his hands than he shone as bright as a motor lamp: but when he stood on his feet again he gave out as much dark as before.

'I don't know that this is going to be much better,' said Joey; 'but at least it's a change. I *wish* I could be just ordinary!'

'You can't be that just yet,' said the little girl.

'Well, thank you very much for the change, anyway,' said Joey.

She stayed and talked to him in the field all day, while he practised standing on his hands, till by the evening he could walk about on them quite as easily as on his feet.

'I think I'll try going home again now,' he said, and said good-bye.

You may imagine how surprised all the village were, to look out of their windows and see a little boy walking up the street on his hands, and shining so bright he lit up the whole place. When he got back home, his father and mother were even more surprised than the villagers had been, and very glad to see him.

But poor Joey's life wasn't any happier. Before, everyone had told him to go away. Now, everyone called to him to come. In fact, the electric light had gone wrong and they found him very useful.

'Joey, dear,' said his mother, 'just walk upstairs in front of me on your hands, will you? I want to fetch a book.' And so it went on till grown-up dinner time, when, instead of sending him to bed as usual, they said: 'Joey, dear, *would* you mind standing in the middle of the table on your hands all dinner time? You will light it up so nicely.'

At that Joey got very cross, and rushed out of the house on his feet darkly.

When he got to the street – '*This* is a new idea!' he said to himself, and started turning cartwheels up the street. Certainly the effect was surprising; for when he was one way up in his cartwheel he was dark, and when he was the other way up he was bright, so he went flashing along the road and flashing through the village, and flashing past the village policeman (who nearly fell down with astonishment), and flashing up to the little girl's house, and flashing into the kitchen. He went on turning cartwheels

three times round the kitchen, even. Meanwhile, the cook was mixing a Christmas pudding, and being, like many other cooks, a very sensible woman, she saw at once what was needed. She fetched a fresh basin, a very big one, and then she seized Joey, while he was still cartwheeling, and popped him in it. Immediately she began to stir, with a big wooden spoon; and she mixed the dark and the light so thoroughly together that presently he got out of the bowl just ordinary.

The little girl had already gone to bed; but anyhow I don't suppose she would have been interested in him any more now he was ordinary. In fact, he never in all his life saw her again.

But his parents were; and when he went home, and his father and mother and brothers and sisters found he was now quite ordinary, and there was nothing by which you could possibly tell him from any other child, they were pleased as pleased as pleased, and often used to tell each other how clever of him it was.

As They Were Driving

As They Were Driving

As they were driving along the road in their coach, they met all sorts of people. There was a tired old man, so they put him in. And there was a tired old woman, and a crane, and a beautiful roller with gold ends, and a gold rug and a silver rug, and another tired old woman. So they put them all in.

Then they found two great, big, beautiful horses. So they took the ordinary horses out of the shafts and made the big, beautiful horses pull, and spread the silver rug over them, and spread the gold rug over the tired old man and two old women and the crane and the roller, and put the two ordinary horses on top of everything.

'Horses!' they cried. 'Don't lie on your backs! You don't look nice.'

And they turned them over.

'Now,' they said, 'we are not afraid of the Stones, even if they do attack us: the Curious Brothers, and the Spotted Mother and Child, and the Fossil Brothers, and the

Plain Brothers, and Mrs Mogany, and the Fierce Mrs Moffadyke, and all.'

Then they met the queen, who was looking very worried.

'I have lost a gold rug and a silver rug,' she said. 'And there's a reward of a hundred pounds for them.'

'Here you are! Here you are!' they cried, and gave them to her.

'Is that all?'

'I have lost a tired old man,' she said.

'Here you are, here you are!'

'And two old women.'

'Here you are!'

'And a crane.'

'Here you are! Is that all?'

'I have also lost two of the biggest and most beautiful horses in the world.'

'Here you are!'

'And I have lost quite the most beautiful roller in the world, with gold ends.'

'Here you are!'

'Now, what reward shall I give you for finding them?'

'I don't know,' they said.

'I do,' said the queen. 'I will give them all back to you for finding them. Here is the crane, and the roller, and the two special horses – '

'Not us! Not us!' cried the old man and the two old women. 'Don't give us back!'

'Stuff and nonsense!' cried the queen. 'You must all be given back to them for finding you. Now,' she said, 'everyone will say how rich you are, driving along with all those things, even if you *do* meet Mrs Mogany, and the Fierce Mrs Moffadyke and all.'

So she went away, and they drove on.

There was a tired old man, so they put him in

The Gardener and the
White Elephants

The Gardener and the White Elephants

There was once a gardener who had to look after such a big garden that he had to get up at one in the morning, and didn't get to bed till twelve at night. In fact, he only got one hour's sleep each night. And working so hard made him get thin and old and rheumaticky and lame long before he should.

One day he planted out a beautiful bed of sweet peas: but when he came in the morning something had been and eaten them up.

'Slugs!' said the gardener; and when he planted out a fresh bed he made slug traps out of orange peel and set them among the sweet peas. But when he came in the morning the sweet peas were all eaten up, but the slug traps weren't touched.

'Then it isn't slugs,' he said; 'I wonder what it is? There is only one thing to do: tonight I must miss my only hour of sleep and sit up and watch.'

So at twelve o'clock he went and sat by the sweet-pea

bed to watch. And he got sleepier and sleepier, till at last, when it was just a quarter to one, he couldn't keep awake and fell fast asleep; and when he woke up all his sweet peas had been eaten again.

So the next night he went to watch again, and this time

took with him his fountain pen; and each time he was just going to fall asleep he gave himself a jab with the nib and woke himself up again. And at five to one, what should he see but a very old rabbit, so old that its fur was all coming off, and its whiskers had turned white, and it hobbled as much as he did. But although it was so old, in a twinkling of an eye it had gobbled up all his sweet peas, and was hobbling away. Then the gardener got up and tried to chase it: but though the rabbit limped he limped too, and, though they both went so slowly, he couldn't quite catch

it: but they hobbled and hobbled till they reached the rose garden; and when they got there the rabbit nibbled a rose leaf, and no sooner did it do that than all of a sudden it became a gay young rabbit again and galloped away at ever such a pace, while the poor old gardener was left rubbing his eyes.

'Well, well,' he said: 'Well, well, well!'

So the third night he went to watch again, and again he kept awake by jabbing himself with his fountain pen, and again the rabbit came, old now as it had been before it ate the rose leaf. It gobbled up the little sweet-pea seedlings, and the gardener chased it: but though he went as fast as he could it was still ahead of him when they got to the rose garden. Then the rabbit nibbled a rose leaf, and quick as lightning it was galloping away. But this time the gardener ate a rose leaf too, and in a moment he was turned into a strong young man, and chased the rabbit as fast as ever he could. This time the rabbit couldn't get quite away, but it was still ahead when it reached its hole. The rabbit dived into the hole, and the gardener dived in after it, and the rabbit burrowed and the gardener burrowed, but still he couldn't quite catch it nor the rabbit quite get away – no, not though it dug like mad. Then, all of a sudden, the rabbit dug its way through into a great black pit, and the gardener, following close behind, suddenly found himself falling head over heels. But he didn't have very far to fall: only, when he sat up, the rabbit was nowhere to be seen.

It was quite dark, but all the same he could just make out some huge white shapes. So he struck a match to see what it was, and found he was among twenty or thirty white elephants, all sleeping on the ground. Then one of them woke up, and asked him who he was and what he was doing.

He found he was among twenty or thirty white elephants, all sleeping on the ground

'I came in chasing that rabbit,' said the gardener. The white elephant looked most shocked.

'What!' he said. 'You were chasing our terrible Lord and Master, the Rabbit Whom None Dares Disobey?'

'Indeed I was,' said the gardener. 'But do you mean to say all you great white elephants are the slaves of one silly old rabbit?'

'Of course we are,' said the white elephant.

'And you do what he tells you?' asked the gardener.

'Of course we do,' said the white elephant.

'But supposing you didn't?' said the gardener. 'What would happen?'

'I don't know,' said the elephant; 'no one has ever dared to try.'

'Then try!' said the gardener. 'Nothing will happen! Do something disobedient and see!'

'But what is there disobedient we can do?' said the white elephant.

'Is there a way out of this cave?' asked the gardener.

'Yes, there is,' said the elephant. 'But the terrible rabbit has told us not to go out.'

'Then come out!' said the gardener. 'Show me the way, and we will all go out together.'

So the first white elephant woke up the others and explained the idea to them. Then they all began to go up the tunnel that led out of the cave together. But they hadn't gone far when they found the rabbit blocking their way.

'Go back!' said the rabbit, and all the elephants were ready to turn round and do what they were told. But the gardener called out, 'I'm not afraid of you! You're only a silly old rabbit!'

'Oh, I am, am I?' said the rabbit in a most wicked voice, and before their very eyes he began to swell and grow, and his teeth grew sharp as a tiger's, and his eyes flashed fire. Then he sprang at the first elephant with a savage growl, and plunged his teeth in its trunk.

'That's what comes of disobeying ME!' he said.

But the gardener was not afraid, and, big and fierce although the rabbit had become, he sprang at it and seized it by the throat, and then began the most terrible fight between the gardener and the rabbit. Sometimes the gardener got the best and held the rabbit down on the ground, and sometimes the rabbit got the best and tried to bite the gardener's throat. But at last the gardener won, and managed to strangle the rabbit till it was quite dead; and then the other white elephants marched on up the tunnel till they reached the open air.

'Now, will you be my white elephants?' asked the gardener.

'We will, of course, we will,' sang the white elephants all together.

Now that he had all these white elephants the gardener, of course, was rich, and didn't have to work in the garden any more. Instead he had a small but comfortable house for himself, and a perfectly enormous stable for all the white elephants: and there they lived happily together for ever after: and this was the strange thing, that though when the rabbit had eaten the rose leaf it had only made him young for one night, when the gardener ate his it made him young for ever, so that he never grew old again at all.

The Man With a
Green Face

The Man With a
Green Face

Once there was a man who had a green face, which wasn't just green, but shone in the dark like a green lamp. So, to make a living, he joined a circus, and nearly all the people in the world paid twopence each to be allowed to see him. But the man the circus belonged to was very horrid, and made the man with the green face very unhappy. The man with the green face was really very ashamed of looking so funny, and hated all the people coming and staring at him, especially because the circus man kept all the twopences, and only gave him just enough food to stop his face losing its green.

The cleverest but one of all the animals in the circus was the elephant, and he hated the circus man too, and hated having to do silly tricks, which weren't really a bit elephantish, but only stupid. So he and the man with the green face were great friends, and used to tell each other their troubles. But the cleverest of all the animals, cleverer even than the elephant, was a mouse; and the horrid circus man was kind to it, because it used to creep about and hide, and tell tales to him about all the other animals, whenever they did anything naughty.

One day the elephant and the man with the green face plotted to run away. But the mouse heard them, and went away and told the horrid man. So he came and locked them both up. He locked up the elephant in a big barn, and shut the man in one of the tents.

The more the elephant thought about being locked up, the crosser he got, and when he got cross he began to push about, till presently he pushed the barn right down flat. Then he went on till he came to the tent where the man with the green face was shut up, and pushed that down, too; and the man got out and climbed on the elephant's back, and they ran away.

They ran and they ran till they came to a level-crossing, and there the elephant stopped to think. He had his front feet one side of the railway lines and his hind feet the other: and he was the biggest elephant in the world. It was night time now, and quite dark. While he was thinking, a train came along. All the engine driver could see was the man's green face, which looked like a green lamp; and on railways a green lamp means 'go on', just as a red one means 'stop'. So he went on, and the train ran right under the elephant. When he found he was going under an elephant, the engine driver was so frightened that he fell off the train.

Then the elephant stopped thinking. He looked at the engine driver and said: 'You'd better come with us.' So the engine driver climbed up on to the elephant's back and drove him instead.

But the train just went on. It went on and oner and oner, till it came to the end of the railway lines. But it still went on, oner, and oner, till it came to the circus, and ran right through it, knocking down most of the tents and waking up the horrid man. But he didn't wake up in time to see it was a train that had got loose that was doing it, for the train went on and left the circus behind. The horrid man said, 'There's that nasty elephant got loose and going racketing around. Mouse, go and tell me what he is doing.'

So the mouse went to look, and came back and said, 'The elephant and the man with the green face have both run right away!'

'Drat them!' said the horrid man. 'We will have to go and chase them.'

So the horrid man and the mouse started off, and on the way they found an old man breaking stones.

'Kind sir, kind sir,' he said, 'help me break these stones.'

'I'll be blowed if I will,' said the horrid man.

And he was. A big puff of wind came and blew him thirty miles. There he saw another old man breaking stones.

'Kind sir, kind sir, help me break these stones.'

'May my neck be stretched if I will,' said the horrid man.

'And so it shall be,' said the old man; 'and you shall be spotted, too.' And he turned him into a giraffe, with a neck as tall as a tree.

So the mouse climbed up it and sat between his ears, and they went on till they caught up the elephant and the man with the green face and the engine driver.

'They won't know who I am,' thought the horrid man, 'now that I look like a giraffe.'

So he went up and spoke to them.

'I'm a giraffe,' he said. 'I've just run away from that horrid circus.'

'Then you'd better come along with us,' said the elephant.

So they all went on together till they came to an orange tree. Then the giraffe reached up his neck, and picked one of the oranges. But they were magic oranges. When he took one bite, his head turned back into the horrid man's head, on the end of the giraffe's neck. Then he took another bite, and his neck shortened, till at last it was only the horrid man's neck on the giraffe's body.

'Look!' cried the elephant. 'It's not the giraffe at all – it's the horrid man!' And he reached out his trunk and snatched away the magic orange and threw it into a river.

Then the horrid man reached up and tried to pick another orange. But his neck was too short now, and all the oranges were too high up. So he had to stay as he was, with a man's head and a giraffe's body.

Then the elephant and the engine driver said, 'What shall we do to punish him?'

'I know,' said the man with the green face. 'Let's start a circus ourselves, and show *him*!'

So they did. And everybody came to see him and paid whole shilling each; and they kept him in a cage. There were soon so many shillings that the man with the green face and the elephant and the engine driver got very rich indeed, and were ever so happy.

But they had never seen the mouse. He crept quietly away, and went off and made his living in other ways.

Telephone Travel

Telephone Travel

There was once a little girl who lived in a tall and not very pleasant house. She was rather a small little girl, being only five years old: and the step-parents with whom she lived were stern and cold to her: they seldom did anything that she liked, or took any trouble to amuse her, so she did not dote on them very much.

She had few toys, and those she had were generally kept locked up in a cupboard: and there was only one thing she could do that was really fun. Some of her step-parents' friends, who were sorry for her, would sometimes ring up on the telephone: then, if she was able to get to the telephone and answer it before anyone else, she would slip quietly down the wire to their house and spend the day with them. (It is true most children can't do this, but she could.) When evening came they would ring up her house again, and she would slip quietly back along the wire the way she had come, and no one ever knew.

One morning, when she was feeling particularly bored,

the telephone bell rang; she rushed to answer it, and without even stopping to ask who it was she rushed down the wire. But a dreadful thing had happened; these were not friends of her step-parents at all, but total strangers who had been given a wrong number. You can imagine how surprised they were when she shot out of the receiver, bumped against their ears, and then tumbled on to the floor: they could hardly believe their eyes, and kept on saying 'My Gracious.'

'You had better stop saying "My Gracious" and send me home. Ring up our house again.'

'But we can't,' said the people. 'We don't know the number: we only got put on to it by mistake. Don't *you* know it?'

But the little girl was too small to know what her own telephone number was. She didn't even know what her step-parents' name was either, so they couldn't look it up in the book.

'Well, there is only one thing to be done,' said the little girl, 'I shall have to stop here and live with you.'

Then she took a look round the room where she found herself. It was the drawing-room, a nice, large, sunny room – probably the best in the house.

'I think,' said the little girl, 'this room would make a lovely nursery. So if you will kindly take this silly, goldy sort of furniture out of it and put in a proper solid sort of table one can jump on and a few dolls' houses and things, I shall be fairly comfortable.'

(This was the way she would have *liked* to have talked to her step-parents, if she had dared: and as these people weren't them it seemed rather a good chance to try what it felt like.)

So the people took out all the drawing-room furniture and put it in one of the attics and lived up there as best

She rushed to answer it

they could, and gave the little girl the large sunny room for a nursery.

That was all right for a bit; but presently she got to know some other children, and then she began to find even this lovely nursery rather small. At any rate, you can't play hide-and-seek comfortably in just one room. So she asked the people to clear out some of the other rooms too, and wisely advised them to put away all their china ornaments in case they got broken.

Soon she had the whole house to play in except the one attic, which she kindly let the people keep.

But presently it got towards Guy Fawkes Day; and, of course, she wanted to have fireworks. But, as it was rather cold, she asked the people if they would mind taking the roof off the house. 'Then,' she said, 'I can stay in the house and let off rockets; I think it would be rather windy in the garden.'

So the people got hammers and started banging away at the inside of their roof, trying to get it off. Soon they had made a quite fair-sized hole.

Of course the neighbours were very much surprised, and asked them what on earth they were doing. So the people told them, and said it was so that the little girl who lived with them could let off rockets without having to go out in the draughty garden.

'You see,' they said, 'she *asked* us to do it; so we must, mustn't we? After all, it's the children who matter, not the grown-ups! One must always do anything one can to make children happy, mustn't one?'

So they went on making their hole larger, and the neighbours were rather sorry for them.

But presently one of the neighbours had a good idea. He came round to the house and told the little girl he had a present for her.

'I hope it's a nice one,' said the little girl: 'I really don't want the trouble of saying "Thank you" if it is nothing much.'

'It's a sixpenny rocket,' said the neighbour.

'Mmmmm,' said the little girl. 'That isn't worth a whole "Thank you," it's worth about half.' So she just said 'Than',' without the ' 'k you.'

However, at last Guy Fawkes Day came, and the little girl sat indoors letting fireworks off into the sky, as they had got practically all the roof off by this time – much more than was necessary.

Then, finally, she thought she would let off the sixpenny rocket that the neighbour had given her.

'This stick is rather heavy, but I suppose it will have to do,' she said, rather crossly, as she fastened the rocket to the people's very best gold-headed walking stick.

Then she set it off. But, as it started, the crook of the walking stick caught in the elastic of her trousers and carried her up into the sky with it.

'Oh dear, oh dear!' cried the people, 'what an unhappy accident! What will beome of her?'

'It's all right,' said the neighbour who had given her the rocket; 'I did it all on purpose. It is a magic rocket; in fact, it is the only thing which knows where she lives, and it will carry her home.'

Which is just what happened. The rocket soared through the dark sky with her and then landed plump in the rain-water tank on her step-parents' roof.

And there they found her and took her out, and washed her, and fed her generally on tapioca pudding and cold mutton, and didn't talk to her, and combed her hair *much* too often.

The Glass-Ball Country

The Glass-Ball Country

In a country where I was once walking there was an enormous castle on the top of a rock. It was all ruined; but it was very difficult to climb the rock, and there was still enough of the walls left to make it quite hard to get in. And inside the walls an old charcoal burner had built himself a cottage, to live there with his wife and his little girl.

At the time he built it there were a tremendous lot of wars. Not just one big war, like we have nowadays sometimes, but any number of little ones going on at the same time and in the same country, so that sometimes you would find as many as three separate battles going on in the same field, and armies falling over each other to get at their own enemy.

The old charcoal burner did not like this, so he thought if he built his cottage up inside the ruined castle, the armies wouldn't find him and he would be out of the way of all these wars. So he built it, and was very careful not to tell anyone where he lived, in case they went and told one of the armies.

But one night late as he was coming back from the town, he met an old pedlar on the high road. The pedlar was very old and wobbly on the pins, and he asked the charcoal burner how far it was to the town.

'Ten miles,' said the charcoal burner.

The old pedlar groaned. 'Dearie me,' he said, 'I don't feel as if I could walk another step.'

Now the charcoal burner was in a great difficulty. If he left the old pedlar, he might die before ever he got to the town; but if he took him to his cottage, he might be a spy, who would tell an army where he lived.

But all the same, he thought it would be kinder to take the old man home and risk it.

So he took him up to his cottage and gave him supper; and then the old pedlar, who was very tired, went to bed.

No sooner was he in bed, however, than the charcoal burner's wife began to row him. 'You silly idiot!' she said. 'I'm sure he isn't a real pedlar at all, but a spy who will tell the armies where we are, and we shall all be killed!'

'Well, let's go and look at him,' said the husband.

So they went up to the pedlar's room and looked at him; and sure enough he had taken off his white beard and hung it at the end of his bed, and was really quite a young man.

'What are we going to do now?' said the charcoal burner.

'We must kill him!' said his wife. 'You go and get your axe, and cut him in half while he is asleep.'

So the old charcoal burner went and got his axe and came back, but when he saw the stranger lying asleep he found it very difficult to make up his mind to do it.

'My axe wants sharpening,' he said.

'Then sharpen it,' said his wife.

So he went down to the grindstone and sharpened and sharpened it till it was sharp as a razor. Then he came back.

'Now do it,' said his wife.

'I can't,' he said. 'You do it.'

So the charcoal burner's wife took the axe, but before she could do anything the stranger woke up, and they only just had time to get out of the room before he should see them.

'Never mind,' said the old woman, 'I will do it as soon as he is asleep again.' But, instead, while she was waiting she fell asleep herself, and didn't wake up till the morning, when the pedlar had already got up and put on his beard and was ready to start on his journey.

But before he went he took a big glass ball, bigger than a football, out of his pack.

'That is a present for your little girl,' he said: 'Thank you for being so kind to me'; and away he went.

'Oh dear, oh dear,' said the old charcoal burner to his wife, 'now he will tell the armies, and they will come and kill us all!'

But the little girl took the glass ball and put it on the mantelpiece, and loved it dearly. And as a matter of fact the stranger was not a spy at all, so it was very lucky they hadn't killed him. But it *did* happen that a few days later one of the armies fighting about the place saw the old castle, and so they said, 'Let's go up there and have a rest, where the enemy won't find us.'

So a whole lot of soldiers began to climb the rock.

'Here they come!' said the old woman. 'Now we shall all be killed. Oh, where can we possibly hide?'

'Haven't you seen there is a whole country inside the

glass ball?' said the little girl. 'It's ever so tiny, only about an inch across: but we might hide there.'

'Good idea,' said her father: so they all three made themselves absolutely tiny and got into the country inside the glass ball. They made themselves so tiny they were just the right size for the country.

Meanwhile the soldiers reached the cottage, and they ate all the food, and put their muddy feet on the beds, and laughed and drank and behaved perfectly horribly. At last one of them said, 'Look at that glass ball: what fun it would be to throw it from the top of the rock, and watch it smash to little bits in the valley below!'

So he took the ball, with the country inside it, and the three people inside the country, and went to the edge of the rock and threw it over. And it fell down, down, down into the valley beneath, where it hit a big stone and was smashed to atoms!

But when the ball was smashed the country that was inside fell out and lay on the ground. It was about as big as a small frog, and first it was hidden under a leaf. But then it began to grow. That was a curious thing; by the afternoon it was quite three feet across. Of course the people grew with it, so they didn't notice what was happening, except that the leaf that at first covered the whole world had now shrunk until it only covered two fields. And all that night the country grew, till by morning it filled all the meadow where it was lying.

Just then a wounded soldier came hobbling along, with another soldier after him trying to kill him.

'Come in here,' called the little girl. So the wounded soldier got into the country, but when the one who was chasing him tried to get in he couldn't do it. And lo and behold, who should the wounded soldier be but the very stranger who had given the little girl the glass ball.

'What country is this?' she asked him.

'It's the Peace Country,' he said; 'no one can fight inside here.'

No more they could. Some of the farmers who were trying to get out of the way of the wars came in, but the armies couldn't.

And still the country went on growing, till now it covered the whole county, and the armies found themselves getting rather cramped for space to fight in. But still they went on fighting and still the country went on growing, till at last there was no room for them at all, and they were all pushed into the sea and the whole lot were drowned. But the Peace Country grew till it covered all the old warry country, and there the farmers and other quiet people all lived together happily, and they made the charcoal burner and his wife king and queen and the little girl princess.

'Now I am a princess,' she said, 'I think I will marry the stranger who gave me the lovely ball.'

But he had disappeared for good.

Nothing

Nothing

When the maid came in to do the dining-room in the morning, 'Good gracious!' she said, 'what a mess those children do leave the table in, to be sure!'

'What have they left on the table?' called the cook from the kitchen.

'Well, there's a drop of milk,' said the maid.

'*That's* not much to make a fuss about,' said the cook.

'There's also a dead Chinaman,' said the maid.

'Never mind,' said the cook; 'it might be worse. Has he just died, or was he always dead?'

'I think,' said the maid, 'he was born dead, and was dead when he was a little boy, and finally grew up dead.'

'What else is there?' asked the cook.

'There's a tooth, and I think it has dropped out of some passing shark.'

'Dear, dear,' said the cook, 'children are *that* rampageous!'

'There is also,' said the maid, pulling up the blind and looking at the table more carefully, 'unless I am much mistaken, a live Chinaman.'

'Tut-tut!' said the cook; 'what a fuss you do make! And was *he* always alive?'

'I don't know,' said the maid. 'And there's a Stocking Left Over From Before.'

'Dearie me!' said the cook. 'What else?'

'Nothing,' said the maid.

'Well,' said the cook, 'don't you touch Nothing.'

So the maid didn't touch Nothing: she cleared away the drop of the milk, and the dead Chinaman, and the shark's tooth, and the live Chinaman, and the Stocking Left Over From Before, but Nothing she left in the middle of the table, and laid the breakfast round it.

Just then the seven children came down to breakfast.

'Why, what *is* that in the middle of the table?' said the youngest, and wanted to play with it.

'That's Nothing,' said the eldest. 'Leave it alone.'

Then the father and mother came down to breakfast too.

'What is there for breakfast?' said the father.

'Amongst other things,' said the mother, 'there's Nothing. Would you like some?'

'No, thank you,' said the father, 'I prefer bacon.'

So he had some bacon, and she had some bacon, and the children ate their eggs.

When breakfast was over, the mother sent for the cook.

'How often have I told you,' she said, 'to throw Nothing away?'

So the cook obediently went up to the table, and picked up Nothing and threw it out of the window.

But she never breathed a word to her mistress about the drop of milk, and the dead Chinaman, and the shark's tooth, and the live Chinaman, and the Stocking Left Over From Before; she hid them under her apron, and when the father and mother were gone she gave them back to the seven children, for she was a nice cook.

'Oh, thank you,' sang the seven children; 'what a nice cook you are!'

So she kissed them all, and then went back to the kitchen.

The Hasty Cook

The Hasty Cook

Once there was a little boy who was rather naughty. One night when he couldn't go to sleep, although he had hardly been in bed half an hour, he got up and said to himself:

'I'll creep down quietly to the kitchen so that nobody hears and cook myself some breakfast!'

So he pulled on a pair of trousers over his pyjamas and crept down to the kitchen; and although it was nearly grown-up dinner time, Cook had gone round the corner to see a friend, so there was no one there.

'I'll see what there is in the larder,' he thought, and went to look. There was nothing but a big bowl of lumps of sugar and a poor dead sparrow. So he went into the scullery to see what pots and pans there were, and when he got there all he found was one big saucepan standing on a shelf.

'That'll do, I think,' he said; and no sooner had he said it than the saucepan jumped off the shelf and came bumping after him into the kitchen.

'Hallo, what are *you* doing?' said the little boy.

'Well, you want me, don't you?' asked the saucepan.

'Yes,' said the little boy, 'get on the fire.'

'If I get on the fire empty,' said the saucepan, 'I shall burn a hole in myself. Won't you put something in me?'

'All right,' said the little boy; and going to the larder he fetched the dead sparrow and the lumps of sugar and put them into the saucepan. Then the saucepan hopped up on to the fire, and soon he could hear bubbly noises coming from its inside.

'Good!' said the little boy; and just at that moment the only button which held his braces on to his trousers burst and shot across the room, and he had to try and find it.

Now what really happened was that instead of finding his own button, he found another one, and the other one was magic, though, of course, he didn't know that. He didn't know how to sew, so what he did was this. He got a piece of fine string and threaded the button on it, then he gathered up the back of his trousers in a bunch in his hand and tied the string round the bunch. Then he buttoned on his braces and went on with his cooking.

'Shall I stir you?' he said to the saucepan.

'No, please,' said the saucepan in a muffled voice. 'I am getting on very nicely, thank you.'

Now a funny thing had begun to happen. The new button on the back of his trousers had begun to grow, and when he felt it with his fingers it was as large as a saucer.

'That's funny,' he thought. 'I didn't remember it was as large as that.'

But still it went on growing, and soon it was so large that one rim touched the floor behind his feet, and the other reached up to the top of his head.

Just then he heard the cook come running in, for the

grown-ups were ringing for their dinner. Then he was
frightened and tried to run away, but the button was so
big and heavy he couldn't; and he only tumbled on his
back *on* the enormous button *on* the kitchen table, unable
to move; and Cook rushed in.

'Well, they *are* in a hurry!' said Cook, as she heard the
bell ringing, and without looking what she was doing she
slapped a dishcover over the little boy and carried him up
on his button and set him on the table. Then, still not

looking what she was doing, she tipped what was in the saucepan into another dish and carried that up too.

When the father took the cover off and just saw his little boy lying on an enormous button instead of his dinner he was so surprised he didn't know what to do. But they soon saw the button was still growing; by now it nearly covered the table.

'Quick!' said the mother, 'there's no time to lose!' And seizing the carving knife she cut the string and set the little boy free. Then she and the father seized the perfectly enormous button and managed with great difficulty to roll it out of the house, and start it rolling down the hill; and they never saw it again. Then she said, 'Let's see what's on the other dish'; so they looked inside and were astonished to find a beautiful birdcage made of sugar, with a sugar bird inside.

'How lovely!' they said. 'But it won't be much for us for dinner.' So they went out and had dinner that night at a restaurant, and they gave the sugar birdcage to the little boy and sent him off up to bed with it.

The Three Sheep

The Three Sheep

Once upon a time there were three sheep, who lived on a high rock. One day one of them said:

'Brothers, I don't like this rock. I shall go somewhere where the grass grows green and the pools are full of wine.'

'Very well,' said his brothers.

So he climbed down off the high rock on to the plain, and he ran across the plain like the wind, and when seven days and seven nights had passed he came to an ivory castle, and at the door of the castle stood a knight all in armour.

'Sheep,' said the knight, 'where are you going?'

'I am looking for a place where the grass grows green and the pools are full of wine,' said the sheep.

'Then come in with me,' said the knight. And he drew from a bag that he carried seven ribands: one was red, and one was blue, and one was yellow, and one was orange, and one was purple, and one was green and one was white; and he bound the seven ribands round the neck of the sheep and led him into the castle. When they passed through the courtyard they came into a great hall, where a king sat feasting, and his throne was all of scarlet wood.

'Sir King,' cried the knight, 'I bring with me a sheep, who seeks a place where the grass grows green and the pools are filled with wine.'

'Then he, too, must wait,' said the king.

Then the sheep looked about him and saw a long table where sat every kind of beast and man; there were white men, and black men, and yellow men. French men and Spaniards and Chinamen and pigmies and Germans and English; there were elephants and lions, and a hippopotamus and a goat and a horse and a unicorn and a weasel, a cat, and a great brown bear; and each sat more still than the others.

Then the knight led the sheep by his seven ribands to an empty seat. And he sat there a day, a month, and a year, he sat there two years, he sat there ten years, and he sat there a hundred years: and at the end of a hundred years a trumpet blew and a beautiful maiden walked into the castle.

'O King, I ask a boon,' she cried.

'Speak on, damsel,' said the king.

'Give me a man or a beast,' said the damsel.

So the sheep rose up and she caught hold of his seven ribands and led him out into the night.

'Where are you taking me?' asked the sheep.

'I am taking you across seven continents and seven seas,' answered the maiden.

So they ran like the wind, till the seven continents and the seven seas were passed over, when they came to a green hill.

'I see,' said the sheep, 'that here the grass grows green

and the pools are full of wine. What do you wish me to do?'

'At the bottom of the hill there is a black castle,' said the maiden. 'Go into that castle, and in each room stamp three times with your feet, and bleat once with your voice.'

So the sheep went down the hill and found the castle. He went into the first room and stamped with his feet, and the echo rang through all the halls. Then he stamped a second and a third time. And then he bleated with his voice, and all the armour hanging on the walls rang. And presently he went into each room in turn, and when he came to the last one, and in each had stamped three times with his foot and bleated with his voice, suddenly the whole castle fell down and vanished like smoke, and the country it was on vanished too, and he found himself back on the rock, where his brothers were nibbling the lichen and the moss.

'Brothers,' he said, 'I have had very strange adventures.'

'Brother,' they said, 'you have never left this rock.'

So a year went by, and the second sheep said:

'Brothers, I do not like this rock: I am going to look for a place where the rivers run with honey and bread grows on the trees.'

So he climbed down on to the plain and he ran like the wind for seven days and seven nights till he reached the Ivory Castle, and the same things happened to him that happened to the first sheep, and the king made him sit in the empty chair for a day and a month and a year, and two years, and ten years, and a hundred years: and then a great trumpet blew and a dwarf marched into the hall. He was very small, and had a hump on his back, and three horns on his head, and he was all black.

'Sir King,' he cried, 'grant me one of your men or one of your beasts to come with me.'

So the sheep rose up and went with him.

'Where are you taking me?' he asked the dwarf.

'I am taking you into the centre of the earth,' said the dwarf.

No sooner had he spoken than the earth opened and swallowed up the dwarf and the sheep too; and for three whole days and nights they fell through the darkness, till they came to a great cavern, where the fires that are in the centre of the earth lick the roots of the mountains. And in the cavern were many other dwarfs, and each had a hammer, and was hammering a piece of brass into some shape or other. One was making an image of a man, and one of a dragon, and one of a sheep, and one of a cross, and one of a lion, and one was not making an image at all, but a machine for something or other.

'I do not see,' said the sheep, 'either rivers running with honey, or bread growing on trees: but what do you wish me to do?'

The dwarf led him to where the fires licked the roots of the mountains, and there was a great glass cauldron full of molten brass set on the flames.

'You must leap into that cauldron,' said the dwarf.

'But I shall be all burnt up,' said the sheep.

'You will not,' said the dwarf, and led him by his seven ribands to a high place from which he could jump into the cauldron, and then the sheep jumped. No sooner did he sink into the molten brass than the cauldron broke, and flames leapt up, tossing the sheep upon their points as if they had been a powerful fountain, and the earth opened above him, and presently he found himself on the rock where the other two sheep were nibbling lichen and moss.

'Brothers,' he said, 'I have had great adventures.'

'Brother,' they answered, 'you have never left this rock.'

So another year passed, and the third sheep said: 'I am tired of this rock, I will go where the birds blossom like flowers and the stars dance ring within ring.'

So he climbed down on to the plain, and began to run like the wind, but not as the others had done towards the Ivory Castle. And after seven days and seven nights he came to a great river, very swift and very black. And floating down the river was a black boat, and in the black boat stood an old man, with a long white beard that reached down till it touched the water. When he saw the old man, the sheep felt that he must follow him; so he plunged into the river, and all that day they were swept along with the current, and with the evening the boat grounded in a shallow bay and the old man stepped ashore, and the sheep landed also. Then the old man came and sat on the sheep's back, and the sheep said:

'Smite me, Lord.'

And he smote him with his hand.

Then the sheep began to gallop with him faster than the wind, and faster than the light of the sun: but presently he said:

'Lord, smite me again.'

And the old man smote him again with the palm of his hand.

At that the sheep began to gallop and fly into the air, soaring on the speed of his galloping, till he had passed through the sky, and came where the birds blossomed like flowers, and the stars danced ring within ring. Then he said to the old man: 'Let us rest here': but the old man

smote him a third time with his hand, and at that all his
strength went out of him, and he fell through the sky like a
falling star, and dropped to earth like a plummet, right on
the rock where the two other sheep were munching lichen
and moss.

'Brothers,' he cried, 'I have had very strange adventures.'

Then the other two sheep looked at him with surprise
and anger.

'Brother,' they said, *'you have never left this rock.'*

The Spider's Palace

The Spider's Palace

Once upon a time there was a little girl who lived in a tangly forest all by herself; and the only thing she was afraid of was the snakes. So she built her nest right on the end of some thin twigs, so thin that the snakes couldn't get along them to bite her, and there she sat in her nest and did her sewing, or learnt lessons out of a book she had, and sometimes played little tunes on a mouth organ; while all the snakes in the forest used to come out along the branches as far as they dared and hiss at her angrily: but they couldn't get to her, and though she was afraid she didn't show it.

One particularly nice and sunny day she was sitting like this, doing something or other, when all of a sudden she had a visitor. He was a big brown spider, and he had let himself down on his rope out of the sky; or so it seemed, for she couldn't see where the rope went to. But he held the end with all his legs and spoke to her kindly.

'Would you like,' he said, 'to leave this little nest where

there are so many snakes about, and come and live in my palace with me?'

'I should be delighted,' said the little girl. 'But how can I get there?'

'Easily,' he said. 'Catch hold of me and I will pull you up.'

So she caught hold of him, and he began to roll up the rope with his legs, and soon they were swinging high up in the air, while all the snakes went to the tops of the trees and waved their heads at them and hissed ten times more angrily now that she was escaping from them altogether.

But still the spider went on winding in his rope, and higher into the air they went, and still higher.

At last, 'Here we are!' he said, and they found themselves on the doorstep of his palace.

The little girl was very much surprised; for truly the palace was a wonderful one. Apart from the fact of its size (and it was one of the biggest there ever have been), and the fact that it was up in the air (its lowest floor being ever so much above the highest mountains), there was one even more extraordinary thing about it: it was absolutely transparent – that is to say, you could see through it in all directions, clearer than through the clearest glass. So that if you were up in the attics you only had to move the rug on the floor and you could see what was happening in the dining-room at least ten floors below. Now the little girl thought, 'This will be great fun'; and so it was, especially when she went to bed at night: for, though the spider shut the door and put out the light, instead of having nothing to do except go to sleep, she could always lean out of bed and look down, down, down, to where the spider sat alone at the head of a large and grand table, eating a grand late dinner by himself: and when he had finished that he used

She would run out on to the clouds and play on them

to walk into the library and smoke a cigar, and it looked ever so funny to see the cigar smoke rise and then flatten out against a ceiling you could see through as plainly as if it wasn't there. In fact, she hardly ever went to sleep at all till every light in the house was put out; and even then there was generally some light on the earth beneath she could look at, or she could lie on her back and stare through the ceiling at the stars and moon.

But there was one room in the middle of the palace she couldn't see into; and this was why. It was covered with curtains. There were curtains over the walls and curtains that drew across the ceiling; and there was even a curtain which drew across the floor, in case anyone went into the cellars and tried to look up. She had often been into the room, and it looked just like any other room: but all the same she knew it was *very* mysterious, because once a week, after dinner in the evening, the spider used to go and lock himself in there and draw the curtains, and stay a whole hour: and what he did the little girl could never find out, although she was the most inquisitive little girl in all the world.

But, all the same, the spider was so kind to her and she was so fond of him she didn't like to worry him by asking too many questions. He let her do whatever she liked, and when she was tired of playing indoors she would run out on to the clouds and play on them. They were rather like hay to play in. Sometimes she used to bury herself while the spider ran about looking for her; but what was even better fun was to climb up a steep cloud and then roll off, head over heels, into the cloud below. When little bits of cloud got down her neck they tickled like mad.

On fine days, of course, when there were no clouds she had to stay indoors – just the opposite of what *we* do on the ground. And sometimes the clouds were too thin, and then she couldn't go out either, in case she fell through; and sometimes they raced by so fast, that if once she had got on them she would never have been able to get back. So she often had to stay in, and then she used to sit and plot to herself how to find out what the spider did once a week in that secret room; though all the same she didn't really want to do anything that would make him angry.

At last she had an idea. When it came to the night for him to go there, she crept quietly out of bed and downstairs. It was very, very difficult, with walls you could see through. If he had looked up from his dinner any moment he might have seen her. But somehow she managed it, and got to the secret room and hid under the sofa: and she had hardly been there a few minutes when she heard him coming. So she flattened herself on the ground and hardly dared breathe.

He walked into the room and she managed to peep out and look at him; and what was her astonishment to see he was no longer a spider at all, but a man! He looked the same sort of man as he had looked a spider: and when she watched him she wondered she could have ever really believed he was born a spider at all, and wasn't a man turned into one; and on the whole she was sorry.

He stayed a man for a whole hour, and then he turned back into a spider and went to bed; and the little girl crept out and went to bed, too.

But, while she was lying awake thinking about it, a queer thing happened. All the clear walls and ceilings of the palace started to go milky: and when she woke up in the morning she couldn't see through them at all. They had all turned into white marble. She got up and went to look for the spider, and, as you might expect, he was now changed back into a man altogether. He didn't say anything, and she didn't either, even when they found the palace had sunk down and was now in the middle of a valley. They neither mentioned the change, and she went on living in the palace just the same. It was a very nice palace as palaces go; but, after all, marble palaces on the ground are much commoner than ones up in the sky that you can see through: and, as I said before, on the whole she was sorry.

The Ants

The Ants

In a little farm near a big wood there lives a farmer with his two sons. He is a very fat old man, and what he likes best to do is to sit by the fire in the evening, dozing. But what his sons like best is to go out into the wood at night poaching. One of the sons is called Harry, and the other is called Will.

One night, Harry came back from poaching alone, and rather late.

'Where is Will, Father?' he asked. 'Hasn't he come in?'

'No,' said the old fat farmer. 'Wasn't he with you?'

'Yes,' said Harry, 'but I lost him.'

They both went to bed; but next morning Will had not come back, nor all that day, and they were rather worried.

That evening Harry went off to the wood as usual; and though the poor old farmer sat up half the night, this time Harry did not come back either.

So the next night the old farmer thought, 'I must go out

and look for those two boys myself.' And he set out for the wood. Now the boys were clever poachers, and knew how to move about the wood at night without being heard: but the farmer didn't, and made such a scrunching and a crackling, treading on dead sticks and pushing through the bushes, that almost at once a gamekeeper pounced out on him.

'What are you doing here?' he asked.

'I'm looking for my two sons,' said the old farmer: 'they used to come to poach in this wood. Have you caught them, by any chance?'

'No,' said the gamekeeper, 'I haven't caught anyone for ever so long.'

'Then, will you help me look for them?' asked the farmer.

'Certainly,' said the keeper, and they started off together to look for Harry and Will.

Presently they came to a little sandy hill in the middle of the wood, with four pine trees on top. They stood there and looked out across miles and miles of tree tops; but they could see no sign of the two lost brothers.

Beyond the hill was a little dell, which was rather steep and difficult to climb into.

'I will go and look in the dell,' said the keeper. 'You wait here. I won't be more than five minutes.'

So the farmer waited five minutes, and then he waited ten minutes, and still the keeper had not come back. When he had waited twenty minutes he said:

'Oh dear, I suppose I shall have to go into this dreadful dell myself.'

He started to scramble, but almost at once he slipped and rolled right down to the bottom. He was not hurt, but he was very frightened, expecting something awful to happen.

At first nothing seemed to happen at all; but then he noticed that everything was getting bigger. The trees seemed to shoot right up into the sky, and to be getting as thick round as towers; the grass grew up to his knees, and then up to his eyes, and soon was towering over his head like a forest itself. A huge pine needle lay in his way, and he bruised his knee badly against it. Of course, what really happened was that he was getting smaller; in fact, before very long he was not quite so tall as one of the little hairs on the back of your hand.

He crept under the wing of a dead daddy-long-legs, wondering what would happen.

All of a sudden an ant came by, and as soon as it saw him it picked him up with its great jaws by the seat of his trousers and rushed away with him. You know the way ants run, not going round things but climbing over the highest thing in their way – so this ant ran now, swinging the poor farmer from side to side and bumping him badly. At last the ant reached his heap, and rushed in, dragging the poor old man along one of the little sandy tunnels. The grains of sand seemed as large to him as big rocks, and scratched and bruised him horribly.

Then they came out into a huge kind of hall. It was very dark, but he could just see rows and rows of ants' eggs, looking like people in white sacks, or beds in a hospital. At the far end sat the Queen; and it was to her the ant carried the old farmer, rushing along at a tremendous pace.

'No time! No time!' sang out the Queen, busily twiddling all her legs at once. 'No time to eat him now: lock him up with the others.'

So the soldier-ant carried him off down another passage, and into a dark little room, and put a heavy blade of grass across the door to stop him getting out. In this room there were also Harry and Will and the gamekeeper, and they all were very sad at thinking how horrid it would be when the Queen *had* got time to eat them, and how sharp and strong her great jaws were.

But the old farmer was full of ideas.

'First,' he said, 'all stand in a row, and then let us each put our head under the coat of the one in front of us, so that we look like one big caterpillar.'

So they did this, and a very fierce caterpillar they looked.

'Now, let us break down the blade of grass,' said the old man. So they all ran at it together, and at last managed to break it down and get out into the passage. Then they began charging down the passage, singing 'God Save the King' at the tops of their voices; and when the ants saw this extraordinary-looking animal coming they fell over each other in wonder and terror, and didn't try to stop them. So they charged along till they came to the great hall, and galumphed through it, knocking over the nurse-ants and banging into the eggs, still singing 'God Save the King'.

'Bite him in half! Bite him in half!' screamed the Queen; and several soldier-ants rushed up to do so. But all the men did was to separate when the ants bit, and then join up again as soon as they could.

'It's no good!' cried the soldier-ants; 'as soon as you bite him in half he joins up again.'

'Oh, *does* he, indeed!' cried the Queen, very angry. 'Then I'll see if *you* can, too.'

She rushed off her throne in a great rage, and began biting the poor soldiers in half with her own jaws. But while she was doing that the farmer and his two sons and the keeper made their way out of the hall by the passage they had been dragged in by.

But alas! They couldn't find their way out of the heap. There were passages running in all directions, and twists and corners everywhere, and soon they were hopelessly lost.

'Oh dear, oh dear!' cried the keeper in despair. 'Now they will get us' – for they could hear an angry murmur as the whole ant army came after them down the passages.

Then – and why it happened no one could tell, but it was really very lucky – they began to swell again. They were soon too tall for the passage they were in, and burst through the ceiling into the room above. And they went on growing, faster and faster, till soon they burst the top off the anthill, and scattered it in all directions. Before long there they were, standing, back at their ordinary heights again, while the poor ants rushed round their feet in the ruins of their palace, trying to save the Queen and the babies in the white sacks.

'Let's go home quickly,' said the farmer, 'before it happens again.'

'Good night!' said the keeper.

'Good night!' said the two poachers and the farmer, and went home.

After that, of course, no one ever went near that dangerous dell again: and though they have gone poaching every night from then till now, nothing has ever happened to the two boys in the other part of the wood, and the old farmer, who is now fatter than any other farmer in the country, is able to sit quietly at home in the evenings, just as he wants, dozing by the fire. If you saw him you would *never* believe he had once been so small that an ant had carried him off by the seat of his trousers.

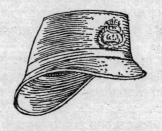

The Invitation

The Invitation

There was once a little girl who slept in a very large room all alone. Sometimes she woke up in the night, and then she would feel very dull at having nothing to do except go to sleep again. So one night when she woke up, she sat up in bed and looked at the moonlight coming in at the window. While she was doing that there was a sudden *Pop!* and the top button of her pyjamas flew off. But, instead of falling on the bed, it floated gently across the room and out of the window; and once it was out of the window, there it stuck in the air, almost within reach. So the little girl got out of bed and went to the window to try and get it back. But, try as she would, she just couldn't reach it. So she climbed on to the windowsill to try and reach farther, and in doing that she tumbled right out.

When she had floated slowly down to the ground she looked about her, but the button was nowhere to be seen. Only the moonlight shone through the trees of the drive, and the wind rustled gently their leaves. For a minute she stood wondering what to do; and then she heard steps coming up the drive, so she hid behind a tree to see who it was. What was her surprise when the steps passed her, and she couldn't see anything at all! Only a postman's cap that floated along about the height of a man's head.

'Well,' she thought, very sensibly, 'I suppose this post-man is invisible, and has an invisible uniform, but he has taken another postman's cap by mistake.'

So she stepped out into the moonlight, where he could see her, and asked if he had any letters for her.

'Yes,' he said, 'here is one'; and putting into her hand an invisible letter he walked away down the drive.

Of course the trouble with an invisible letter is that you can't read it, so the little girl was rather worried what to do. At last she decided she would go and see her very best friend, who was one of the gateposts down at the end of the drive. So, holding the letter very tight (because if she dropped it she would never be able to find it again), she walked down the drive after the postman, and climbed on to her friend.

'Dear gatepost,' she said, 'do help me to read this letter.'

And immediately the letter became visible, and she read it.

'*Dear little girl,*' it said, '*we are giving a party in our castle tonight. Will you come?*'

That was all: it didn't say who it was from, or where the castle was, or anything. Now the little girl knew the country round well, and there wasn't any castle there anywhere. That is to say, at any rate there were none on the ground; there might be some in the air – that she didn't know. So she climbed a tall tree to have a look.

At the top of the tree there was a railway station, with a train just going to start: so she got in, and away the train went across the sky till it came to another station, and there she got out.

'Can you please tell me the way to the castle?' she said to the stationmaster.

'Which castle?' he asked. 'There are nine near this station.'

So she showed him the letter. He scratched his head.

'Well,' he said, 'that's the queerest letter I ever have seen, so I expect it comes from the queerest castle. And *that* one is only just round the corner.'

So he told her the way to go, and she soon came to it.

It was indeed the queerest of all castles, for it was upside down.

The gate was at the top, with big towers below it, and a flag at the bottom.

'Well,' she thought, 'I suppose the best way to get in is to turn upside down too.'

So she did, and soon found herself walking in at the gate quite comfortably.

The party that was going on in the big hall inside was a simply lovely one. Each person was dressed all in one colour, and these colours were of the brightest. There would be one person in bright lilac, and another in blue, and another in peacock, and another in green, and another in yellow, and another in orange, and another in scarlet, and another in crimson. They all nodded to the little girl and told her they were glad she had come. The ones who were talking walked about the floor, but if they wanted to dance they did it on the ceiling, where there was more room, and if they wanted something to eat they walked up the walls to little tables which stuck out here and there.

Presently the little girl found a nice man to dance with, so they went up to the ceiling and danced round and

round the electric light. Then they walked down the wall to one of the little tables and there ate ices.

'What will you do,' he asked presently, 'when the Special Licence gives way?'

'What is the Special Licence?' asked the little girl.

'It is a sort of spell,' he said, 'giving leave for the castle to be upside down. And it gives way at one o'clock – why, it's nearly one o'clock now!'

'Oh, I'll wait and see what happens,' said the little girl

very sensibly, and began hurriedly to eat another ice before the time should be up.

When it struck one, the first thing that happened was that all the people shrank and shrank and turned into mice; but they still stayed their lovely colours, and chased each other round and round the little girl, looking very pretty. Next the castle got smaller and smaller, and finally came to bits till there was nothing left but a single bit of broken china; and the mice all ran away.

'Thank you very much,' she called after them: 'I *did* enjoy myself.'

Then the little girl found she was at home, and sitting under the kitchen table.

So she stole quietly up to bed again, and luckily no one heard her.

The Three Innkeepers
or
The King's Legs

The Three Innkeepers

or

The King's Legs

There was once a farmer who got tired of farming, so he thought he would go to the town and start an inn.

But when he got there, he found that there were two inns there already: and one of them was called *The King's Head*, and one was called *The King's Arms*.

'Very well,' he said, 'I shall call *my* inn *The King's Legs*.'

So he had a beautiful sign painted with the King's legs on it, and hung up outside.

Now this turned out very well. Nobody had ever heard of an inn being called *The King's Legs* before, so all strangers used to come in out of curiosity, to ask why on earth the inn had got such a strange name. Then, of course, they had at least to buy a drink, and sometimes they stayed the night so as to be able to use note paper with such a lovely address when writing to their friends: and so *The King's Legs* inn became the most prosperous in the town, and the new innkeeper got rich and the old innkeepers began to get poor.

So they put their heads together, and wondered what was the reason. 'I know,' said the landlord of *The King's Arms*. 'It is because he has got such a funny name for his inn. I'm going to change the name of mine.'

So he decided to call his inn in future *The King's Stomach*; and he took down the old sign to get a new picture painted. 'Mind you make it a big one,' he said to the sign painter, 'or else it won't look royal' – though, as a matter of fact, the king of that country was not particularly fat at all.

Then he hung up the new sign and waited to see what happened.

But what happened was not at all what he expected. Some courtiers of the King happened to be travelling that way; and, when they saw the sign, they were very angry and shocked. 'What!' they cried: 'The impudent creature! Fancy calling *that* great fat stomach the King's! As if everyone didn't know he had the slimmest and most elegant little stomach in the kingdom!'

'What shall we do?' asked one of the courtiers. 'Shall we arrest him for high treason and have his head cut off?'

'We might do that,' said another of the courtiers. 'But, on the whole, wouldn't it be more fun just to throw some stones through his windows?'

The others all agreed; so they got off their horses and began throwing stones through the windows of *The King's Stomach* inn until there wasn't a single pane of glass left unbroken. Then they rode on.

So the landlord said to the landlord of *The King's Head*: 'Well, *my* plan didn't work very well. Have *you* got one?'

'Yes, I have,' said the landlord of *The King's Head*. 'I have thought of a very funny idea.' He went and bought a curious sort of gilt bird, and shut it up tight in a glass case, and put a label on it, 'Weathercock,' and put it in the window of his inn.

Now it wasn't long before some people came by. 'Hullo,' they said, 'that's a funny thing to do, to keep your weathercock shut up in a glass case where the wind can't get at it! I wonder why he does that?'

So they went in to ask.

'Why do you call that funny gold bird in a glass case a "weathercock"?' they asked, when they had ordered some beer.

'Because,' said the landlord, 'just what it is, *whether cock* or hen, I can't decide.'

Lots of people came in to ask the same question, and he gave them all the same answer.

So now the landlord of the new inn, *The King's Legs*, found all the people going back to *The King's Head*, and himself not getting rich any more.

So he got a large gilt egg, and went along quietly at night, and slipped it in the glass case along with the bird.

Next day some people came by and asked the usual question and were given the usual answer.

'But, you silly old ass!' they cried out to the innkeeper, 'anyone can see it's a hen! Why, it's laid an egg!'

And they were so angry they took up several of the big glass beer tankards that were about and started hitting the landlord with them on the head. It didn't hurt his head much because it was very hard, but it broke all the tankards, and he went along to see his friend about it all.

'It's a funny thing,' said his friend, 'but whatever we do it always seems to end in glass being broken.'

'That means,' said the other one, 'there must be some sort of magic in it all.'

'Well, in that case,' said the first one, 'we had better go and see the Village Witch, and ask for her advice.'

So they went to the Village Witch, who happened to be also the District Nurse.

'There is only one thing to be done,' said the witch. 'We must kill him.'

'Well, will you do it for us if we pay you?' asked the innkeepers.

'Certainly,' said the witch, and putting on her nurse's uniform she bicycled round to *The King's Legs*. There she found the landlord in the parlour at the back.

'Dear, dear!' she said. 'I am sorry to hear you are so ill.'

'Am I?' said the landlord: '*I* hadn't heard.'

'Perhaps not, but *I* had!' said the witch firmly: 'You had better go to bed.'

So he went to bed, and she nursed him a bit and then said she would come back the next morning to see how he was.

The next day she came in the morning and went up to his room, looking very sad.

'You can't think,' she said, 'how sorry I was when I heard you had died in the night.'

At that the innkeeper looked very pale and frightened.

'What!' he said. 'Died in the night! Are you sure? Nobody told me.'

'No,' she said firmly; 'but they told *me*! I'll send the undertaker round this afternoon to measure you for your coffin.'

As it happened the undertaker was busy that afternoon and couldn't come: but he came the next morning.

'Good morning,' he said, 'I have come to bury you.'

'What!' cried the innkeeper, who was just as clever as the witch; 'hadn't you heard?'

'Heard what?' said the undertaker.

'Why, I was buried yesterday afternoon! When you didn't come, I got the undertaker from the next town, and *he* buried me.'

The undertaker was very sorry at that because he didn't like losing a job, but there was nothing to be done if the innkeeper had been buried already: so he just went away.

Then the innkeeper got up and dressed and went down and started serving drinks in the bar. Presently the witch and the two other innkeepers looked in, to see if he was safely buried yet.

When they saw him quite well and serving drinks they were very upset.

'Good gracious!' exclaimed the witch, 'what are *you* doing here?'

'What!' exclaimed the innkeeper. 'But surely you must have heard! I am the new landlord of *The King's Legs*! They buried the last one yesterday afternoon, poor chap!'

At that the two other innkeepers and the witch were so upset that, without saying a word, they all three ran hand in hand down the village street to the village pond and drowned themselves there: and the landlord of *The King's Legs* got a small paintbrush and wrote on the bottom of his sign in white paint:

Under Entirely New Management.

Inhaling

Inhaling

Once there were two children out for a walk by themselves, when they saw an enormous policeman. He was at least six times as big as any other policeman in the world.

'I know what's happened,' said the girl. 'He's been inhaling too much!'

'What's inhaling?' said the boy.

'You know,' said the girl, 'when we have a cold, and they pour some funny-smelling stuff into a jug of hot water, and make us breathe over it. That's inhaling.'

'Quite right, miss,' said the policeman, in a six-times-big voice, 'I have been inhaling too much: *much* too much! Would you like some of the stuff?' And he gave them a small glass pot.

'Thank you,' she said. 'We're rather small, you see: there'd be no harm in trying a little.'

So they went home.

That night, when they were both in the bath, they

poured some of the stuff into the hot water of the bath and immediately began to sniff it.

'This is fine!' said the little boy: '*Aren't* we growing nicely?'

And so they were; they were soon as tall as grown-up people. But the only trouble was that nurse, who was giving them their baths, was swelling too; and as she was big to begin with she was now enormous.

'Put your head out of the window!' cried the boy. So the nurse did, and then, of course, she stopped smelling the stuff and stopped growing.

But the children didn't. They stood in the bath and got taller and taller.

'This ceiling *does* hurt my head,' said the girl.

And no wonder, for they were pressed hard up against it.

All of a sudden *crack!* went the ceiling, and pop! came their heads up into the room above! This room was their father's study, and there he sat working.

'Bless me, children!' he said, when he saw their heads coming up through the floor. 'What will you do next?'

'I don't know, Father,' said the girl, whose face was now above the top of his writing table.

'Bless me!' he said again. 'What a funny smell!' – for the smell of the stuff began to come up through the hole in the floor.

On that, of course, he began to swell too.

'Bless me!' he said. 'Fancy starting to grow again, at my age!'

And indeed he was soon about twice his ordinary height.

Just then the boy's big toe got caught in the chain of the bath plug and pulled it up, and all the water ran away, and the magic stuff with it, and so no one grew any more.

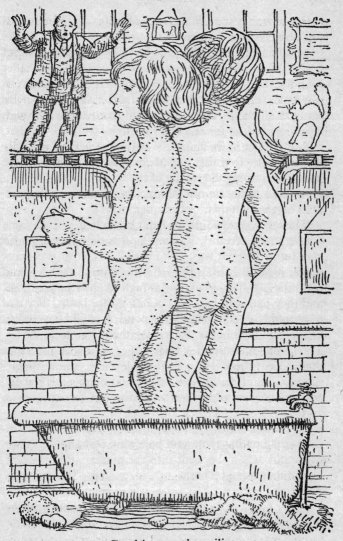

Crack! *went the ceiling*

But now they were in a great difficulty. The mother was still ordinary size, because she hadn't been there. And the nurse hadn't had time to grow very much before she put her head out of the window; but even then she was taller than the tallest soldier you ever saw. As for their father, he was twice the size he had been, and couldn't sit in his study at all comfortably, and could hardly crawl through the door. But as for the children, they were so big that, with their feet in the bath, the bathroom ceiling was only just up to their waists and their heads were just on the point of bumping the ceiling of the study above.

'What a funny family we are,' they said, 'with the children bigger than their father and mother!'

'However,' they said, 'we can't go on living in the same house, that's certain'; so they built a new house, and a very funny house it was. The nursery, of course, was enormous; it reached from the cellar right up to the roof, and the nursery table was almost as high as an ordinary room, and they had washbasins as plates. As for baths, they had to go and have cold ones in the pond; it would have taken *much* too much hot water to give them one in the house. Then came the study for their father, that was just about double size: there was a double-size table, and a double-size chair, and double-size books, and double-size papers, and double-size pipes and matches and tobacco boxes, and double-size pictures and even a double-size waste-paper basket. But the poor little mother had just an ordinary-size drawing-room and bedroom, and had to be ever so careful, when she went into the nursery, that the children didn't tread on her.

But as for the swollen nurse, it was much less trouble to send her away and get a new one of the ordinary size, so that's what they did.

The China Spaniel

The China Spaniel

There was once a school that was rather cross and dull, and it was run by one old woman.

Now it so happened that one of the children at this school was a china spaniel, the kind that has a gold chain round its neck, and doesn't look as if it had much sense. As a matter of fact, this one had practically no sense at all: he was easily the stupidest pupil in the whole school, and could never learn his lessons properly.

One day they were all given some poetry to learn for homework; and the china spaniel really did try his hardest: but when he came into school the next day he couldn't remember a single line of it.

In fact, the only thing that came into his head to say was:

Pink and green silver-paper toffee-paper!
Pink and green silver-paper toffee-paper!
Pink and green . . .

'What!' screamed the old woman: '*That* isn't what I gave you to learn!'

But there must have been some sort of magic in the words, for immediately all the other children in the school, the good ones and the clever ones and everybody, rose up from the desks, and all began chanting together at the tops of their voices:

> Pink and green silver-paper toffee-paper!
> Pink and green silver-paper toffee-paper!

— and out into the street they all rushed, dancing and singing at the tops of their voices.

'What's this? What's this?' said a policeman. 'What's all the row about?'

'Pink and green silver-paper toffee-paper!' shouted the children.

And thereupon the policeman began to dance too, and chanted it with the children.

'What's this? What's this?' cried the Chief of Police, who happened to be passing: 'One of my policemen dancing? What does this mean, sir!'

'Pink and green silver-paper toffee-paper!' replied the policeman: and no sooner did he hear it than the Chief of Police started chanting it too, with all the rest, for by now there were quite a lot of other people of the town who had joined the procession and went along chanting

> Pink and green silver-paper toffee-paper!

with the china spaniel, who had started it all, marching proudly at their head.

At last they came to the Royal Palace, whereupon the King came out on his balcony ready to make a speech.

'My loyal subjects, I see you gathered together before my palace in great numbers. Well, as you know, I am a

I am a kind king

kind king and always anxious to give you what you want, so what is it?'

'Pink and green silver-paper toffee-paper!' cried the people; 'pink and green silver-paper toffee-paper!'

'*What* did they say they wanted?' whispered the Prime Minister, who was a little deaf, at the King's elbow.

'Pink and green silver-paper toffee-paper?' asked the Prime Minister's secretary in polite surprise.

And then, in a twinkling, they were all dancing and

chanting and shouting in the palace as well as outside it:

> Pink and green silver-paper toffee-paper,
> Pink and green silver-paper toffee-paper,
> Pink and green silver-paper toffee-paper,
> Pink and green silver-paper toffee-paper,
> Pink and green silver-paper toffee-paper,
> Pink and green silver-paper toffee-paper!

Nor was it long before the whole nation was singing it: and some enemies who were besieging the town at the time, hearing it, thought it must be some sort of national anthem, till they found themselves starting to sing it too; and, in short, it wasn't long before the whole world was singing it – the whole world, that is to say, except the old woman who kept the school.

'It would take more than the whole world going mad,' she said very firmly, 'to make *me* start dancing and playing the goat!'

And she went on trying to run her school just as before it happened, the silly old thing.

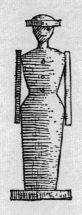

The Magic Glass

The Magic Glass

There is a little boy I know who always looks very carefully in wastepaper baskets, 'because,' he says, 'you never know what valuable things you may find that some silly grownup has thrown away.'

One day he found what looked like the glass off the end of an electric torch. 'That will make a most useful magnifying glass,' he said, and put it in his pocket.

That night he woke up; and not being able to get to sleep again he thought he would look at a few things through his glass. The first thing he looked at was a wooden rabbit lying on the end of his bed; but the strange thing was that, when he looked through the glass, instead of the toy, what he saw was a real live rabbit, sitting up on its hind legs and wobbling its nose at him! Then he took the glass from his eye: and lo and behold, it was only a wooden one again.

'This *is* a funny glass,' thought the little boy.

Then he looked through it at a china duck there was on

the mantelpiece: and, sure enough, there was a real duck, which would have jumped down on the floor if he hadn't quickly taken the glass from his eye and turned it back to china again.

By this time the little boy was so excited with his glass that he got out of bed and crept down to the room where his father and mother were lying asleep. 'For,' he thought, 'if it turns toys into real, I wonder if it turns real people into toys?' And he put it to his eye and looked at his father and mother. And so it was: they were immediately wooden Mr and Mrs Noah out of the Ark. To make sure, he took a pin, and keeping the glass firmly in his eye he tried to stick it into his mother. But it wouldn't go in, for she was now quite hard: it only scratched a little paint off. Then he took the glass away, and they were his mother and father again. But just to make sure he stuck the pin in again. This time it went right in, and his mother sat up with the most awful yell.

'You naughty boy!' she said. 'What are you doing out of bed? And *what* did you stick a pin into me for?'

'I'm awfully sorry, Mother,' he said, 'but I thought you were Mrs Noah! You were, a minute ago, you know!'

'Mrs Noah?' said his mother. 'Stuff and nonsense! You must have been dreaming! Go back to bed at once.'

So he went back to bed, and soon was asleep. In the morning, when he went to school, he put the glass in his pocket.

Now, on the way to school there was a dog which the little boy simply *hated*. Every day when it saw him coming it used to poke its nose through the gate and growl and bark, and he never knew when it might jump out and bite him. So when he got near, and the dog began to bark, he looked at it through his glass, and all at once it turned into one of those funny china dogs you see sometimes on the mantelpiece in cottages. So the little boy picked it up, and threw it on the ground, and smashed it to bits. He wondered very much what would happen, now that it was smashed, when he took the glass away from his eye. What *did* happen was that it turned into a nice fur rug. So he hid it behind the fence. 'Good!' he thought: 'I'll pick it up on my way home and give it to Mother, to make up for jabbing her with that pin.'

When he got to school he forgot about the glass till halfway through lessons, when he took it out of his pocket and looked at the mistress through it. Immediately she turned into a golliwog.

The little boy was not very surprised, but you may imagine all the other children were! They made such a noise in their astonishment that the head mistress came into the room, and hearing her coming he slipped the glass back into his pocket.

'Now then, children!' she said, 'what's all this noise?' (It wasn't a very nice school.)

'The mistress has just turned into a golliwog!' shouted the children.

'Nonsense!' said the head mistress, who was a very cross old woman; but just then the little boy looked at the mistress again through his glass, and turned her again into a golliwog.

'Good gracious me! What's this?' said the head mistress, and went up to take hold of the golliwog: but when she got close, of course, the little boy could see her through the glass too, and immediately she turned into a Dismal Desmond.

At that, of course, the children were awfully pleased, and wanted to have them to play with: but the little boy said no, they mustn't go near or they'd all be turned into dolls, and all the other children said how clever the little boy was to have done it. So he kept on looking at them till lesson time was over; and then he went home, not forgetting to pick up the fur rug to give his mother.

That night, when he was in bed, his mother remembered his trousers wanted a button sewing on, so she came upstairs and fetched them, and then she found the glass in his pocket, and took it downstairs with her.

'What a funny glass!' she said, and put it to her eye, and looked at herself in the looking glass.

That was a most awful thing to happen: for not only did she turn into wooden Mrs Noah immediately, but the glass simply became a painted glass in Mrs Noah's eye. And so she would have to stay, because the wooden Mrs Noah, of course, couldn't move, and as long as she didn't move she was staring at herself in the looking glass, and, as long as she stared at herself, Mrs Noah she would stay.

As a matter of fact she was Mrs Noah all night, and still Mrs Noah when the maids came down in the morning to sweep the room.

'There's that naughty boy left one of his toys in the drawing-room,' they said, and went to move it: but as soon, of course, as they moved it away from the looking-glass it turned back into a person.

'Good gracious!' they said. 'It's the mistress!'

And she rubbed her eyes, and said she felt very sleepy because she had sat up all night. Meanwhile the glass rolled away into a corner, and happened to stop just in the mouth of a mouse hole, and no one thought of it any more.

That afternoon the little boy's mother had a whole lot of people coming to tea. They were very stiff and grand people that the little boy didn't like at all; but all the same he thought he would creep downstairs to the drawing-room and have a look at them. So he did, and watched them from where he couldn't be seen. But the little boy wasn't the only inquisitive one. Just at the same moment the little mouse came up his hole, and thought he would have a look at them too: and across the hole was the magic glass, so he looked through that.

Immediately all the people turned into the funniest lot of dolls you have ever seen: dutch dolls and wax dolls and rag dolls, and even china ornaments. And that wasn't all. There were some pictures on the wall which the mouse could see, too: and while the real people turned into toys,

the people in the pictures all stepped down into the room, in their funny old-fashioned dresses, and started to eat the tea. At that the little boy was so pleased that he laughed and clapped his hands, and the noise frightened the mouse, who ran away into the back of his hole, and so all was as before.

But presently the mouse came back and thought he would have another look. Just then the little boy's father came in from the office, and was standing in the drawing-room door when all the people turned into toys again, and the pictures started once more coming out of their frames. Meanwhile, the mouse was so excited he kept turning round to tell the other mice what he was seeing, and then looking back, and then turning round again, so that the boy's father was nearly astonished out of his wits, seeing them turn from people into toys and toys into people again as fast as the wink of an eye. But at last the mouse went away: and then they all stayed people, and when the tea party was over went home as if nothing had happened.

But the little boy's father was really rather frightened. 'There's something magic about this house,' he said to himself; and as soon as he could he found another house, and they all went to live in that and left the old one empty.

But no one noticed the magic glass sticking in the mouth of the mouse hole: and if someone else comes and lives in that house, and the mouse comes up his hole to have a look at them, I suppose the same thing will happen to them!

The Christmas Tree

The Christmas Tree

It was Christmas Eve, and the Christmas tree was all decorated ready for Christmas Day. But no sooner had everyone gone to bed than the toys hung on the tree began to talk to each other.

'What fun it would be,' they said, 'if we all got down and hid.'

So they all climbed down off the tree, leaving it quite bare, and went and hid – some behind cupboards, and some under the hot-water pipes, and some behind the books on the shelves in the library, and anywhere they could think of.

In the morning the children came down, wishing each other a Happy Christmas: but when they saw their lovely tree all bare, without so much as a cracker left on it, they cried and cried and cried.

When they heard the children crying the toys all felt thoroughly ashamed of the naughty trick they had played: but all the same they didn't quite like to come out of their hiding places while anyone was about. So they waited till everyone had gone to church and then they slipped out.

'I know!' said the Noah's Ark, speaking in all his voices at once, 'I have an idea!'

So he led the other toys out of the house, and into the town, and there they separated and found their way into every toy shop and sweet shop there was, by the back door. Once inside, they invited all the toys and all the sweets to come to a grand party they were giving, and led them back to the house.

'Here is where we are giving the party,' they said, pointing to the Christmas tree. So all the new toys climbed up on to the boughs of the tree and hung there. Indeed, there was hardly room for them all, for now there were ten times as many as there had been before.

All through church the children went on crying quietly behind their prayer books, and came home feeling still very sad; but when they saw their Christmas tree with ten times as many presents on it as there had been before, and ten times as many candles, all kindly lighting each other, they laughed and clapped their hands and shouted with joy, and said they had never seen such a lovely Christmas tree in all their whole lives.

They had never seen such a lovely Christmas tree

The Old Queen

The Old Queen

Beyond the farthest mountain that you can see there lies a country, which is perfectly flat, except for one mountain in the middle of it (which was not always there), and a small hill. On that small hill there is a palace, and in the palace there lives a queen. She is so old that no one can even remember when the King her husband died. She just goes on reigning and reigning. This is the story of why she never dies.

Once upon a time a very long while ago when the Queen was young, she was walking with the King her husband in the garden of the palace.

'Let me give you a present,' she said. So she picked an apple and gave it to the King.

'Now *I* must give *you* a present,' said the King, and going to the chicken run he took out of it the only egg that was there.

'Here is my present,' he said to the Queen.

'That is a nice present,' said the Queen; 'I will keep it next to my heart.'

So the Queen took the egg, and put it down the front of her dress to keep it warm. And at night she took it to bed with her; and in the morning when she put on her clothes she put it in the front of her dress again. And so at last the egg was hatched, but instead of a chicken the most marvellous bird came out of it; its feet were grey, and made of stone, and its feathers were green, and made of leaves, and its beak was shining, and see-through like water. So the Queen took it to show the King.

'That is the greatest wonder in my kingdom,' he said.

'It all comes of your giving me that egg,' said the Queen.

'And that came of your giving me the apple,' said the King.

'And that came of our walking in the garden,' said the Queen:

'So let's walk there again.'

So they went out into the garden, with the bird perched on the Queen's shoulder. When it felt the sunshine it began to sing, and its song was like all the rivers in the world falling off all the rocks in the world. To hear it made the King and Queen so happy they said:

'Let's go and ring the church bells.'

So they went to the church, and began to pull the bell ropes; but however hard they pulled, not a sound could they hear.

'That is funny,' said the King, and looked up to see what was wrong. And to his surprise he couldn't see the top of the steeple at all: it was stretching up high into the sky, right out of sight.

'They must be so far off by now that we can't hear them.'

'When I was a little girl,' said the Queen, 'my nurse told me that if I pulled a bell rope, and then when the bell began to ring I hung on, it would lift me up and up into the air. Let's try and see what happens.' So they each gave a good tug to their bell rope, and then instead of letting go they hung on, and the bell rope lifted them up into the air. But instead of going down again it carried them on, up and up, and all the while the wonderful bird flew round them singing its song, now round their heads and now round their feet, though they were three hours altogether going up.

First they could hear the bells faintly ringing in the distance.

'We are getting near them,' said the King.

Then as they got nearer the sound got louder and louder, till at last it was so loud they couldn't hear their lovely bird sing; and yet, when they were on the ground they couldn't hear the bells at all. Then they reached the bells themselves, and they climbed out on to the tiptop of the church steeple. They were so high up they couldn't see their country at all: it was all blue down below like the sky, and far down there were clouds floating under their feet.

The point of the steeple was sharp as a pin, but on top was a weathercock. So the King sat on the arm which said West, and the Queen sat on the arm which said East, and the bird on the arm which said South.

'I wish there was someone to sit on the arm which says North,' said the Queen: and no sooner had she said it than lo and behold there was a fairy sitting on it as if she had been there all the time. And the fairy was green, and shiny and see-through like the bird's beak.

'Come and see my country,' said the fairy.

When she said that, one of the clouds which were far

Lo and behold

under their feet began to rise up, till soon it was close under them; and then they found that though it looked like cloud it was as solid to walk upon as ground. So they walked with the fairy till they came to her house; and the house was made of green cloud, and inside was a hearth, but the fire, instead of burning yellow or red, burnt a bright blue.

'Now,' said the fairy, 'I am going to make for each of you a magic robe, so that once you have worn it you will never die. But while I do it one of you must be blowing the fire.'

'*I* will,' said the Queen, and took the bellows. Now the curious thing about these bellows was that when you blew with them instead of air coming out it was water; and yet instead of putting the fire out it only made it burn the brighter.

'But someone must help me with these scissors,' said the fairy; 'they are far too large for me to manage alone.'

And so they were, for each blade was as long as a tall man.

'*I* will,' said the Queen. 'I understand scissors better than he does.'

'Then he must blow the fire,' said the fairy, 'I can only work while it is being blown.'

So the King took the bellows and began to blow the fire, but not looking what he was doing, watching the Queen and the fairy instead. Then the fairy took off a peg a piece of stuff so magic I mustn't describe it; and the Queen took hold of one handle of the scissors and the fairy the other and they made a robe for the Queen and she put it on.

'Now let's make one for the King,' said the fairy.

And they began to do it. But now, for the first time, the King began to look at what he was doing; and when he saw water pouring out of the bellows – 'Good gracious!' he thought, 'that will put the fire out' – so he stopped blowing.

No sooner did he stop blowing than the cloud broke under them, and both he and the Queen began to fall.

'Don't be afraid!' said the bird, flying under them. 'You sit on my back.' So they did; and when they did, the bird changed into a mountain, the mountain that is there now; his feathers became trees, and his feet became rocks, and his beak became a waterfall.

As the King and Queen were walking down the side of the mountain she said to him: 'Now I will never die and you will: and that is the saddest thing that has ever happened to either of us.'

But every year they climbed the mountain, and planted flowers on the top in memory of their lovely bird. Forty years went by, and the King grew old, and the Queen grew old, and the King at last died: but the Queen didn't, she just went on getting older and older, and she is still alive now.

The School

The School

Once there was a schoolmaster and a schoolmistress who hadn't any school.

'This is absurd,' they said. 'We *must* have a school': so they got a brass plate, and wrote the word 'SCHOOL' on it, and put it up on their gate.

The next day they rang a bell at nine o'clock in the morning for lessons to begin. But of course no one came. So for half the morning he taught her, and for the other half she taught him.

The next day he said, 'I am going out to see if I can't find someone to come to our school.' On the way he passed a toy shop, and in the window there was a fine big Noah's Ark; so he bought it and took it home. Then he took out Mr and Mrs Noah, and Shem and Ham and Japhet, and all the animals, and put them in the desks in the schoolroom.

'Now,' he said, 'we have got a splendid big class to teach!'

So all that day they taught the things out of the Ark.

'I do think this is a well-behaved class,' said the school-mistress. 'They sit ever so still and never make any noise at all!'

Which was perfectly true. They never made a sound. The only trouble was that when you asked them a question they still didn't make a sound, but just sat quiet and didn't answer.

'What do two and two make, Noah?' the schoolmistress asked.

But Mr Noah said nothing.

'Next!' she said.

But Mrs Noah said nothing either.

'Next! Next! Next!' said she. But Shem and Ham and Japhet and the two lions and the two elephants and the two mice and all the other animals said nothing either.

'What *I* think,' said the schoolmistress, 'is that we've got the stupidest class that ever was!'

So she popped them all back in the Ark and went out to look for something else.

Presently she came to a shop called 'Railway Umbrellas'. It was where they sell all the things people leave in railway carriages and never come back for: umbrellas, and handbags, and bananas, and babies, and concertinas, and parcels, and so on. So she went in. And sitting in the window she saw a dear little black kitten.

'Is that a railway kitten, too?' she asked the man.

'Yes, madam,' he said. 'Somebody left him in a basket on the rack of a train only the other day.'

'Well, I'll have that one then,' she said, and bought it and took it home. When lesson time came they took all the creatures out of the Ark and made the kitten sit in the middle of them.

The naughty Railway Kitten

'What do two and two make, Railway Kitten?' she asked.

'Meaow!' said the kitten.

'No, they don't, they make four!' she said. 'What is the capital of Italy?'

'Meaow!' said the kitten.

'Wrong! It's Rome. Who signed Magna Charta?'

'Meaow!' said the Railway Kitten.

'Wrong again,' she said., 'it was King John! I've never even heard of Mr Meaow!' And she turned round and started to write a sum on the blackboard. But as soon as her back was turned the naughty Railway Kitten began to have a lovely game with all the wooden creatures out of the Ark. He knocked them down, and sent them skidding all over the floor: and when the schoolmistress looked round again he had climbed on his desk, dipped his tail in the inkpot, and now was swishing it about so as to flip ink all over the room.

'Oh, you *naughty* kitten!' she cried. 'If you're not good I'll send you back to your railway!' And she took him and shut him up in the kitchen.

Just then the front-door bell rang, and the schoolmaster went to see who it was. Outside there was a little girl, with a packet of school books under her arm.

'Please,' she said, 'I've forgotten the way to my school; may I come to yours instead?'

'Certainly! Certainly!' said the schoolmaster. So she came in, and hung her hat and coat on a peg, and changed her shoes, and went and sat down in the school-room.

Now, not only was she as good as the Ark creatures, and sat perfectly still and quiet, but also when she was asked a question she answered it, and always got the answer right. And she never once let the Railway Kitten play during lessons, though out of lesson time of course she played with him a lot, and gave him his saucer of milk.

When the evening came she said: 'Is this a boarding school? Because if it is I don't think I shall bother to go home.'

'All right,' they said, and put her to bed.

Now, as I have told you, all day she had been good as good: but when she went to bed there was just one thing she was naughty about: she WOULD NOT get out of the bath when she was told. When she had been washed she just lay on her back and refused to move, and the poor schoolmistress simply *couldn't* make her. She lay there till the hot water turned her as pink as a lobster, and it wasn't till the water had got quite cold that she would come out. Then, of course, she was cold too, and shivered, and her teeth chattered when she got into bed.

The next day she was perfectly good again: but when night came the same thing happened – once she was in her bath she *would not* move.

'I am going to count one – two – three, and then pull up the plug!' said the schoolmistress. 'ONE – ! TWO – ! – '

And before she could say THREE the little girl jumped out in a terrible fright.

'That's a good plan,' thought the schoolmistress, 'I'll do it again.'

And so she did. Every night, when the little girl wouldn't get out, she counted ONE, TWO, and before she could say THREE out she jumped. And this went on for a whole week. But when it came to Saturday night, and she counted ONE! TWO! all the little girl said was 'SHAN'T!' and lay so flat on the bottom of the bath that only her nose was above the water.

'THREE!' said the mistress, and pulled up the plug! Away the water rushed, down the waste pipe: and alas!

away went the poor little girl with it. First her feet were sucked into the hole, and then her legs, and then her body, and in a moment she had disappeared altogether.

'OH, what *have* you done,' cried the schoolmaster. 'You have lost our only child!'

'I don't care!' said the schoolmistress in a stern voice. *'She should have got out of the bath when she was told!'*

If you have enjoyed this book and would like to know about others which we publish, why not join the Puffin Club? You will receive the club magazine, *Puffin Post*, four times a year and a smart badge and membership book. You will also be able to enter all the competitions. For details of cost and an application form, send a stamped addressed envelope to:

The Puffin Club, Dept A
Penguin Books Limited
Bath Road
Harmondsworth
Middlesex